BOOKS
for
BOYS

ROBIN HOOD'S BEST SHOT

IAN WHYBROW
ILLUSTRATED BY TONY ROSS

Hodder
Children's
Books

a division of Hachette Children's Books

For Daniel Jerome Shaw – a fine young reader!

A Catalogue record for this book is available
from the British Library.

ISBN-13: 978 0 340 91797 8

Printed in the UK by CPI Bookmarque, Croydon, CR0 4TD

The paper and board used in this paperback by Hodder Children's Books are natural
recyclable products made from wood grown in sustainable forests. The manufacturing
processes conform to the environmental regulations of the country of origin.

Hodder Children's Books
A division of Hachette Children's Books
338 Euston Road, London NW1 3BH
An Hachette Livre UK Company

Robin Who?

Hello there, young reader! Are you ready for a story about a hero of mine? And you don't want any stuff about kissing and cuddling? Don't worry! This is going to be a proper adventure story with a bit of . . .

GALLOP!

. . . a bit of . . .

TWANG!

. . . and plenty of . . .

HOORAYS!

Here we go then. But first let me ask you a question. What was the second name of the famous hero called Robin who dressed in Lincoln green? (Now be careful!)

Are you thinking, "What a daft question and the answer is 'Hood'"?

Or are you thinking, "Aha! I know the answer to that *trick* question! Robin Hood's name was really Robin Goodfellow! So the answer isn't 'Hood' but 'Goodfellow'"?

Well, either answer will do. When Robin Goodfellow was grown up, he became an outlaw and everybody called him Robin Hood.

Back to my story, then. I am going to tell you just how Robin Hood was given that famous nickname. And then you'll be able to tell all your friends.

But hang on a minute. Talking of names, let me remind you about some of his Merry Men. Because we must not forget that they weren't always merry *men*. For quite a long time they were merry *boys*. So here we go.

Danny's Wonderful Nose

When you think of Robin Hood, I
expect you think of him calling up
his Merry Men by blowing his horn,
a bit like this . . .

But most people don't think
about him when he was a boy and
he looked like this . . .

He was a strong and daring young fellow. And when you live in a manor house with creepers growing up the wall, what is the point of just walking up the stairs to your bedroom? It's a lot more fun going up the hard way. Robin Goodfellow always liked a challenge!

Let's just think for a minute
about the Merry Men before *they*
grew up. Who was the merriest of
all the Merry Men? Friar Tuck, of
course! And how did he get his
name? Some people think it was
because he liked *tuck*. He was
always *tuck*ing in to a chicken leg
or a slice of
pie! So
when he
was
grown
up, he
always
looked round
and jolly –
like this . . .

But really it was because
his name was Daniel
Tucker.

Yes, honestly this was
what he looked like as a
boy. A skinny little chap
he was. He was always
laughing and he loved
reading. Robin thought
the world of him. He
used to say that Danny taught him
more about nature than he'd ever
learned in a classroom.

Danny grew up on a farm not
three miles from Goodfellow Hall
where Robin was born, and he
knew just about everything about
animals and nature.

He had a wonderful sense of smell and he could tell you the name of any herb or flower just by its perfume! Remember that wonderful nose of his. It's going to come in handy later.

More Merry Men and Boys

Who shall I introduce next among Robin's famous Merry Men? Will Scarlett, I think.

He was a clever, handsome young man and famous for being a good fighter. His enemies would come charging at him, waving their swords and Will Scarlett would do a quick swish with his quarter staff, like this . . .

. . . and a quick bash like that . . .

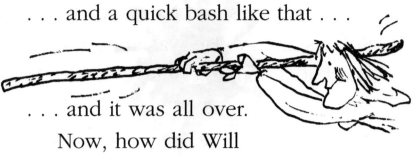

. . . and it was all over.

Now, how did Will Scarlett get his name?

Some say it was because he always wore a scarlet waistcoat. But I will tell you the real reason. He was the son of a blacksmith who lived in a village on the edge of Sherwood Forest, and his family name was really Bartlett. But Robin gave him the nickname Will Scarlett because of his bright red cheeks and his red-hot temper!

And have you heard of Alan A-Dale? He was one of Robin Hood's

bravest fighters and he made all
Robin's arrows. He was almost as
good at shooting a bow as Robin. In
all the stories about Robin Hood,
Alan plays his lute and sings "Hey
Nonny Nonny" like this . . .

But I will tell you something
much more interesting. He was
brilliant at throwing his dagger.
How do you suppose that could
come in handy? We'll see if you're
right later on.

Introducing Big John Little

There's just one more of
Robin Hood's best friends
that I should mention.
John Little was his name.
Have you heard of him?
Well, turn his name around. *Now*
you know him – Little John! He is
famous all over the world as the
strongest and tallest of all the Merry
Men who lived in Sherwood Forest
and wore Lincoln green.

Even as a boy, John was enormously tall and strong, with proper muscles that stood out on his chest and arms. So why was he called Little John? Keep reading and you'll find out.

John Little was born seven or eight miles from Goodfellow Hall, in the city of Nottingham itself. His father and mother were servants to a rich and powerful merchant who was also the Mayor.

One day, the Mayor and his wife arranged a birthday party for their cruel and spiteful son, Lucas. It was very expensive and they had it in the garden of their mansion. They  called in entertainers, minstrels and jugglers. They hired a silly Fool to make the children laugh, and as a special treat, they had a dancing bear. Lucas spent the afternoon poking the poor creature with a stick and calling it names.

He was showing off, just to make his spoiled little guests laugh. The torment became too much for the bear. He broke his chain and charged about the yard, growling and knocking over the tables and chairs.

The Mayor ordered his men to kill the beast with their spears or to shoot their crossbows at him.

"Stop, Mr Mayor, stop!" cried young John Little. "Let me try to calm him!" He ran and caught the terrified beast. Then he threw his mighty  arms around the bear and wrestled him to the ground. All the time he whispered to it, "Steady, my poor lad. Go steady now! You need fear nobody here!" Within a few minutes, he had the bear eating nuts from his hand, as soft and gentle as a puppy.

Everybody cheered John Little for making the bear tame again. They called him a brave hero and a

mighty wrestler. That made Lucas
jealous and angry! He stamped his
foot. Then he crept up behind John
and cracked him over the head with
his stick. "Back to the kitchen where
you belong, servant boy!" he
screamed, hot with rage.

There was a sudden
hush. John Little just
smiled. He took the
stick from Lucas and broke
it in pieces. Then he lifted
Lucas right up in the air
above his head. He was
about to throw him into
the middle of the pond
to cool off when the
Mayor rushed forward.

"Stop! Put my son down at once!" he commanded.

John did as he was ordered.

"Punish that horrid, rude boy, father!" panted Lucas. "Have him whipped!"

The Mayor could see that most people in the garden thought that this was very unfair. Even the most spoilt children were looking upset. He took his son to one side and said quietly to him, "He certainly deserves to be whipped for his bad manners." Stroking his dark moustache, he went on, "But I have a suggestion. This young giant may be strong, but surely he will never match your skill with the longbow.

After all, you have had the best teachers that money can buy."

"No boy in the county can beat me at archery!" declared Lucas proudly, tossing his head.

"Then make him a challenge!" whispered the Mayor.

Lucas spoke out, so that all the crowd heard. "John Little, you have insulted me. I therefore challenge you to an archery contest on May Day. If I win, my father will have you flogged and throw your parents out into the street to starve!"

One or two people in the crowd started to mutter. They knew that Lucas practised shooting arrows every day! John Little was too busy for sports. So to make it sound fairer, Lucas went on. "My father agrees that if, by any chance you win, you will escape punishment and your father and mother may stay and be our servants on double pay."

The rich children clapped loudly.

They thought Lucas was very generous.

"You know I am no archer, Master Lucas," said John. "I shall have very little time to practise."

"Nonsense! You will have three whole days!" said the Mayor. "What are you afraid of?"

"I fear nothing," said John, grimly. "I shall face your challenge."

"An archery contest we shall have, then!" announced the Mayor. "It will be held at the deer park on May Day! I shall arrange for notices to be displayed everywhere.

All the people in the city shall see what an excellent archer I have for a son. And that is very important, because one day you will be—"

"Sheriff of Nottingham!" cried Lucas. "I shall be the richest and most famous Sheriff of Nottingham ever! And you, John Little, can expect very *little* from life!"

"I may never be rich, Master Lucas," said John quietly. "But there are many ways for a man to make a name for himself!"

And how right he turned out to be!

Robin Hears About the Challenge

Three days later, very early on a bright spring morning, Robin and his friends, Danny, Will and Alan, were riding their horses along a track at the edge of Sherwood Forest. They had spent a happy hour watching baby badgers rolling and playing in front of their set.

Trust Danny, with all his woodcraft, to know just when and where to see such a sight!

"Ah! Smell that woodbine," he said, lifting his nose like a hound.

"Do you mean honeysuckle? I smell nothing," said Will and Alan.

"Whoa, Proudfoot!" said Robin, stopping his fine white horse for a moment. Then he said, "You have a marvellous nose, Danny! What's the secret of your keen sense of smell?"

"There's nothing to it," smiled Danny. "Lift your face like this, open your nostrils, and draw up the air slowly, like water from a well."

Robin threw back his head and breathed the air slowly and deeply, just as Danny had said. "Ah, I have the scent! It's coming from that grove, far over there. Very sweet it is too. But what else can I smell? Who had garlic for breakfast?"

"Well done, Robin!" chuckled Danny Tucker. "You have picked up the scent of wild garlic. Some call them ransoms. They are excellent food for the blood. Delicious in a salad!

27

But I am surprised that you can smell them! For I am sure that the nearest clump of ransoms grows down by the stream. Why, that lies at more than a hundred paces from this spot! Your nose must be as sharp as mine!"

"Nonsense!" said Robin modestly, but he was pleased by the praise.

Danny turned his horse and galloped off to the spot he was talking about. It really was a hundred paces away. He jumped down and pulled a bunch of ransoms. "For my supper!" he called.

Meanwhile, Alan and Will had wandered under the shady branches of a giant oak. "Have you seen the

notice fixed to this tree?" Alan said
to Robin. It read . . .

YE LORD MAYOR OF
NOTTINGHAM INVITETH ALL
YOUNG PEOPLE OF YE COUNTY
TO ENJOY AN AFTERNOON OF
SPORTS AND GAMES AT YE
DEER PARK ON MAY DAY AND
TO WITNESS A CHALLENGE
MATCH IN THE TARGET
SHOOTING BETWEEN THAT
BRAVE YOUNG GENTLEMAN
LUCAS AND HIS SERVANT
BOY, THE GIANT JOHN LITTLE

"Lucas is no brave gentleman. He's a spoilt brat!" said Robin. "But I wonder who this John Little is."

"I have heard of this so-called Giant Little!" said Will. "They say he almost drowned Lucas in his father's fish-pond on his birthday! That is the reason for the challenge." Will's cheeks flushed with anger. "And by St George, I could drown that toffee-nosed coward  myself! For I hear that he crept up behind John Little and struck him on the head with a stick!"

"And it is a pity that he and his ma and pa must soon be begging

for their daily bread," said Alan.
"For I hear tell that if Lucas wins the
match, the Mayor will throw them
out of his mansion."

"Most unfair," said Danny. He
had ridden back to join his friends
with the garlic-smelling ransoms
tucked in his pocket.

Robin swung his trusty longbow
off his shoulder. "One hundred
paces you say?"

"As far as that fence post," said
Alan, pointing.

In a flash, an arrow was notched on to the string. Robin looked along it, pulled on the string and *whoosh*! How that arrow flew! A second later, there was a sharp crack. The fence post was split clean in two!

"I think I should enjoy an afternoon of sports and games this May Day afternoon," smiled Robin. "Are you with me lads?"

"Hooray! We're with you, Robin!" cried Danny, Alan and Will.

A Sad Parting

When May Day came, John Little kissed his mother and father goodbye. The Mayor would not allow them to go to the deer park to watch their son shoot arrows. They had to stay at home and polish the silver.

"How are your fingers?" asked his father.

"Not too bad," said John. He was too brave to say how raw and sore they were from the rubbing of his bowstring. He had spent every spare moment he had trying to improve his archery. Now, at one hundred paces, he could hit a target six or seven times out of ten.

"You must not blame yourself if you fail, John," said his mother. "For Father and I and will always be proud of you."

"I shall do my best!" said John. "That is all a chap can do! And with a bit of luck, we shall all sleep in our proper beds tonight!"

At the Deer Park

Robin, Danny, Will and Alan enjoyed themselves at the May Day Games that afternoon. They tried for the longest leap and Robin took the prize – a cake. He cut it exactly in four and shared it with his friends.

 Guess how Alan won a gingerbread boy? By dagger-throwing, of course. (I told you it would come in handy!) Will got wet bobbing for apples. "Look," said Danny, "that apple has red cheeks just like yours!"

"Oh, go and climb a slippery pole!" snapped Will.

"Very well then, I shall!" said skinny Master Tucker. A brave effort he made too. He got almost to the top but just couldn't hold on.

Down he slid, grinning all the way. "Now that I'm all mucky, I'll have a go at 'Catch the Greased Piglet'. Who will lend me a halfpenny?"

A halfpenny was found. Off went Danny to try his luck at the mucky sport. He ran as fast as his legs and his spirit could carry him. But the piglet was too slippery for him! Danny didn't give up. Instead, he knelt down, put his hands to his face and started to make squeaky little grunting noises. The piglet stopped in his tracks.

"Oink?" said Danny, sounding just like a sow calling her babies. That did the trick. The piglet came trotting over to answer the question and Danny grabbed him.

Robin and his friends were laughing merrily at this clever trick, when they heard a posh voice behind them. "It takes a pig to speak a pig's language, I see!"

It was Lucas with a crowd of rich town boys, on his way to the archery contest.

"Haw haw haw!" sneered Lucas's supporters.

Danny didn't mind. He tucked the piglet under his arm, smiled and chucked the creature under the chin. He never lost his smile. "Wave hello to your cousin Lucas!" he called, and waggled the piglet's front trotter. That changed Lucas's tune pretty quickly!

"What, you cheeky young pup, Tucker?" screamed Lucas.

"Now, now, make up your mind, Lucas. Is Daniel a pup or is he a piglet?" said Robin. "I hope your eyes will serve you better when it comes to shooting arrows at a target!"

It was the turn of Robin's friends to laugh.

Lucas was furious. "Make no mistake, Robin Goodfellow," he snarled. "John Little and his family will be sleeping in the gutter tonight! I shall be the winner!"

A trumpet sounded. It was the signal for the challenge match to start!

John Little v Lucas

A huge crowd gathered behind the ropes to see the challenge match. The target was set up at exactly one hundred paces, between the two lines of trees they call the Long Walk.

42

Lucas was dressed in the finest
silk clothes. He had six bows to
choose from. He tested every string
before choosing a wonderful
weapon that stood taller than he.
His trainer offered him a leather
quiver full of arrows.

Alan whistled with admiration.
"Peacock feathers!" he whispered.
"Only the best for Master Lucas!"

There was still no sign of John.

"Where can he be?" people said.

Lucas turned to them. "He's lost his nerve and run away, I expect!" he sneered.

"I do not think so!" declared Robin. "If he's as big as they say, he's probably in the wrestlers' tent. There's so much noise in there, he won't have heard the trumpet. Let me try." He raised his horn to  his lips and blew. At the sound of the horn, the crowd saw the flap of the wrestlers' tent fly open.

Out ran a huge, strong lad, his long straight hair streaming behind him.

"I'm surprised they call you little, John," joked Robin. "Good luck, Little John!"

Little John? *Little* John? A big chap like that? The name spread like wildfire among the crowd. They loved the joke. "Little John!" they began to chant. "Little John! Little John!" And the name stuck!

Now, reader, I should like to be able to say that Little John scored ten bull's-eyes out of ten. But the truth is, he fired his ten arrows, but he only hit the target twice.

Still, the giant boy had a giant heart. He put out his hand to shake with Lucas. "You won, Master Lucas, fair and square. I'm sorry that I was no match for your excellent shooting. Well, you may be sure that the Little family will annoy you no more."

"Exactly!" crowed Lucas. "I want you out of our house before I reach home."

Little John put out his right hand to say well done.

"Don't try to mock me! I will not shake hands with a servant boy!" cried Lucas.

"Then perhaps you will allow *me* to shake his hand!" The words were Robin's. He had jumped over the rope and joined the two archers.

"You did mighty well, Little John. For I see that you made your own bow and feathered your own arrows. That is more than Master Lucas did! Well done!" He shook the giant boy firmly by the hand.

"Get away, Goodfellow!" yelled Lucas. "Or I shall call my father. He'll give you the thrashing of your life!"

"Only a coward lets his father fight his battles," said Robin. "If you have any courage, you will answer a challenge from me!"

"What are you talking about?" asked Lucas.

"I challenge you to hit that target from here – blindfold."

"What nonsense!" laughed Lucas. "No-one can do that! It's a hundred paces away!"

"Well, I think *I* can do it," said Robin. He raised his voice. "And before the good young people of Nottingham, I challenge you to try."

The crowd began to cheer.

"You're just boasting!" said Lucas.

"I will let you have three tries to my one," said Robin. "If you win, you may have anything of mine that you want. If I win, you must ask your father the Mayor to take back Little John's father and mother. He must pay them twice as much as he did before. Then they will be able to pay for him to go to school and learn reading and writing—"

"And archery!" joked Little John.

"That too. What do you say, Lucas?"

"I will agree," said Lucas cunningly. "But if neither of us hits the target, you must give me anything of yours that I ask for."

"Very well," said Robin.

"Then I will have Proudfoot," said Lucas.

The crowd gasped. Everybody admired Robin Goodfellow's magnificent white horse. He was as dear to Robin as a brother. Robin went pale as a ghost.

Robin's Hood

"Forget the challenge," said Little John. "You don't even know me. We have never even met before. You must not risk Proudfoot for me. You owe me nothing."

"I owe you a lot," said Robin. "You have shown me how to smile, even when you have lost everything. That is a lesson worth paying for.

51

But don't worry, I shall not lose
Proudfoot." He turned to the
Mayor's son. "Now Lucas – the first
three arrows are yours!"

Lucas was not a stupid boy.
Before he could be blindfolded, he
looked long and hard at the target,
before taking aim. He fitted a
peacock arrow on the
string of his best
bow. "Now you
may blindfold
me," he said.
Danny took
off his scarf

and tied it tight round Lucas's eyes
as he stood ready to fire.

TWANG! WHIZZZ! THUD!

"Ahhhh!" sighed the crowd.

Lucas's arrow missed, but not by much. "I have two more arrows! You must keep your word!" he cried. Again, he took off the blindfold, and took careful aim before he allowed himself to be blindfolded again.

TWANG! WHIZZZ! THUD!

"Ahhh! He just missed by a whisker!" said the crowd.

For the last time, Lucas prepared himself.

TWANG! WHIZZZ! THUD!

"Ahhh! *Just* over the top!" shouted the crowd.

"You are only allowed one shot, remember!" Lucas told Robin. In his mind he saw himself riding through the streets of Nottingham on Robin's precious milk-white horse.

He imagined crowds of boys and girls running out of their houses to cheer him. "Hooray for Lucas! Long live Lucas, Sheriff of Nottingham!"

Robin's voice woke him from his dream. "Will you let Daniel Tucker run down to the target and point to the bull's-eye?" he asked.

"Why?" exclaimed Lucas. "You'll be wearing a blindfold!"

Danny was wondering what Robin was doing, but whatever it was, he trusted Robin with his life. Off he marched. One hundred paces down the Long Walk towards the target.

When he stood beside it, Robin cupped his hands and shouted, "Place a ransom in the centre."

"What ransom? What are you talking about?" said Lucas. "No tricks now. Somebody get me a blindfold."

A pretty young maid ran out of the crowd. "Will this do?" she asked. "It is the hood from my robe."

"Lincoln green! Perfect!" smiled Robin. "I shall wear this with pride." The maid pulled the hood tight over Robin's eyes.

"Can you see at all?" asked Lucas.

"Of course not," said Robin.

"I do not cheat!" He raised his voice. "Are you ready, Danny?"

"The ransom will not stay in the middle of the target, Robin!" shouted Danny.

"Get out of the way!" shouted Lucas. "He must shoot now!"

Daniel Tucker was not going to let Robin down. Bravely, he leaned across the target. He held the leaves of the wild garlic between his finger and thumb and placed the little bulb of the plant on the bull's-eye.

"Shoot when you are ready!" called Danny. "Don't worry about me!"

"Get back! You could be killed!" cried the pretty maid.

A steady breeze was blowing up the Long Walk. Robin lifted his face. He opened his nostrils under the green hood. He drank the air deep. It was just as if he was drawing water from a well. He found the smell he was seeking. He felt for an arrow from his quiver and placed it on the string.

He lifted the bow and pulled
back with all his strength.

TWANG!

Many children in the crowd closed
their eyes.

WHIZZZ!

"Look out, Danny!" yelled the
crowd.

THUD!

"Oh no!" cried the crowd as
Daniel Tucker fell to
the ground.

They charged together up the Long Walk to where he lay. When they reached the place, one hundred paces from the shooting line, they were silent.

They turned Danny over. "There's no sign of the arrow!" someone said.

"Yes there is," said the pretty maid who had lent Robin her hood as a blindfold. "It is here. It has gone through a plant and it is right in the middle of the target!"

"BULL'S-EYE!" roared the crowd.

And so it was, reader. Poor Danny had only fainted. It was the shock. But he was quite all right. Robin's wonderful nose had smelled exactly where the wild ransom was, in the very middle of the target.

Loud Cheers!

HOORAY for Robin's marvellous nose and for Danny, the future Friar Tuck, who showed him how to use it.

HOORAY for Robin's skill with his bow that let him find a target he could only smell!

HOORAY for the breeze that carried the smell of garlic one hundred paces to Robin's nostrils.

HOORAY for Proudfoot, safe in his stable at Goodfellow Hall.

HOORAY for Little John and his mum and dad who got their jobs back on double pay.

And HOORAY for Maid Marian. Yes, reader, it was Maid Marian who let Robin borrow her hood! And it was because of her that England's greatest hero got his name!

Shall we have a bit of kissing and cuddling? No fear! Just three toots of the horn for Robin Hood and all his Merry Men!

And finally, three boos for that big cowardy custard, Lucas, the boy who would soon become the Sheriff of Nottingham!